NIAN

THE CHINESE NEW YEAR DRAGON
— A BEASTLY TALE —

ADAPTED FROM A CHINESE LEGEND

VIRGINIA LOH-HAGAN ILLUSTRATED BY TIMOTHY BANKS

PUBLISHED by SLEEPING BEAR PRESS

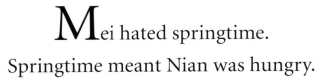

Mei hated springtime.
Springtime meant Nian was hungry.

Nian was the fierce dragon that used to rule the land until a magical warrior put a spell on him. Because of this spell, Nian was forced to hide in a mountain under the sea. But every spring, Nian came out to fill his empty stomach. He especially loved to eat little boys and girls.

Mei was scared. Her whole village was scared.
They could hear the rumbling of Nian's stomach.
That's how they knew winter was over and spring was coming.

The night before the first day of spring,
the magical warrior visited Mei in her dreams.

The warrior said to Mei, "Hundreds of years have
passed and a new year is coming. Nian's power grows
stronger. And my spell grows weaker each year.
I can no longer keep him in the mountain under the sea.
You must defeat Nian. You must do this in fifteen days
or Nian will be free forever. My cane will help you."

Mei asked, "Why me?"

"You were born in the Year of the Golden Dragon.
It is your destiny."

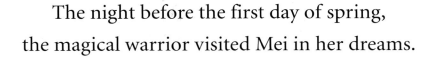

When Mei woke up the next morning, the magical
warrior's walking cane was next to her pillow.

"Mei!" MaMa yelled. "Wake up!
Nian is on his way. We must flee and hide!"

MaMa herded the animals into the barn.
"Hurry! Nian will devour anything in his way.
He'll eat our livestock and crops. With his large
mouth, he can swallow many villagers in one bite."

Mei had lost her father and little brother
to Nian's mighty jaws the year before.

Mei helped MaMa hide. But then she remembered
the warrior's cane and ran to get it. "I'll be right back."

Mei stopped in her tracks.

She heard a terrible roar and
smelled a terrible smell.

Nian made his way toward Mei.
She could see his sharp teeth and claws.
She could see his long, slimy tongue.

Mei grabbed the cane.
She also grabbed a cooking pot
and banged it with the cane.

She yelled,
"Nian, go away!
You are not wanted here!"

Nian covered his ears with his big paws.
He didn't like the noise.

That gave Mei a wonderfully noisy
idea. She yelled to the other villagers,
"Make a lot of noise!"

The villagers obeyed.
They banged pots.
They clanged pans.

They hollered.
They hooted.
They threw
firecrackers at Nian.

Nian fled back to his
mountain under the sea.

For five days, the villagers were happy.
They drummed their drums and gonged their gongs.
They whooped and hollered. They laughed loudly, really loudly.
Just in case Nian was listening.

The villagers thanked Mei by giving her
a beautiful red silk robe.

Mei was wearing the flowing red robe when she heard screams and roars. Nian had returned, even hungrier and angrier than before! He had packed his ears with cotton to block out noise.

Mei didn't have time to run. She threw a lantern at Nian. She covered herself with her red robe. Nian shielded his eyes from the redness of the robe and the brilliance of the fire. He backed away in fear.

That gave Mei a wonderfully bright idea. She said to the villagers, "Wear your brightest reds and shine your brightest lights!"

The villagers obeyed. They wore their reddest clothes. They hung red banners on their windows and doors. They placed bright lanterns everywhere. Mei cut a piece of her red robe and made a flag, which she attached to the magical cane. She waved it to shoo Nian away.

Nian fled back to his mountain under the sea.

For five days, the villagers were delighted. They dyed all their clothes red. They burned fires all day and all night. Just in case Nian was watching.

On the tenth night, the magical warrior once again appeared in Mei's dreams.

"Nian is coming back and he wants revenge. Be very careful.
Remember, you only have five more days to defeat him."

Mei knew she had been lucky the first two times. This time she needed a plan.
So she came up with a wonderfully tricky idea.

Mei took all the food in her house, put it in red bags, and stuffed them into a scarecrow. She dressed the scarecrow in her old clothes. She placed the scarecrow in front of her door. She told the villagers to do the same.

The villagers obeyed.

At the last minute, Mei shoved the warrior's cane inside the scarecrow.

On the fifteenth day, Nian returned.
He had covered his eyes with long eyelashes
and packed his ears with cotton.

The dragon stormed into the village.

His jaws chomped on the scarecrows that had been filled with food.

But when he got to Mei's scarecrow, he choked on the cane.
The cane then magically turned into a leash.

The magical warrior from Mei's dreams
suddenly appeared.
He captured Nian with the leash.

"Nian is conquered.
He'll never be evil again.
You've brought us good luck and fortune,
Mei. You've fulfilled your destiny.
Now I'll fulfill mine."

The magical warrior mounted Nian and together
they turned into a stone statue in the middle of the village.

The villagers were overjoyed that Nian was defeated,
and they held a party in Mei's honor!

They put food offerings in front of their houses.
They lit lanterns. They threw firecrackers. They
dressed in red. Some villagers dressed up as Nian
and did a dance. They celebrated a new year
without fear of the dragon!

"*Gong Xi. Gong Xi.*
Congratulations! Congratulations!"
The villagers heralded
their heroine, Mei.

Nian never harmed the villagers ever again.

From then on, at the start of every spring, the villagers celebrated Mei chasing out Nian. They made a lot of noise. They wore a lot of red. They lit a lot of lanterns.

And every spring, Mei gave a food offering to the statue of Nian and the magical warrior. Just in case . . .

Chinese New Year is celebrated on a different day each year based on the lunar calendar, or moon cycles. It occurs in late January to late February. It is also known as the Lunar New Year or Spring Festival. People spend fifteen days preparing for it. On Chinese New Year Day, people attend lion dances and parades. For fifteen days after, people continue to celebrate. The Lantern Festival marks the end. (To learn more about the Chinese New Year, read *PoPo's Lucky Chinese New Year*.)

The Legend of Nian [*nee-anne*] tells the story of the origins of Chinese New Year traditions. The Chinese word for "year" is "nian." A phrase for celebrating Chinese New Year is "Guo Nian." It means "the passing of the beast." Another phrase used to celebrate the Chinese New Year is "Kuo Nian." It means "surviving the beast."

This legend explains why Chinese people take fifteen days to prepare for the new year. This is because it took fifteen days to get rid of the beast, Nian. During Chinese New Year celebrations, people give food offerings, wear red clothes, put up red banners, throw firecrackers, and make a lot of noise. In the legend, people did these things to scare away Nian. Today, it means people want to chase away bad spirits and bring in a lucky new year. The Lantern Festival and lion dance remind people of chasing Nian away. Celebrating a new year also means people were strong enough to endure the previous year.

There are different versions of this legend. But in all the stories, Nian comes out every spring to attack a nearby village. A powerful male (usually a monk or warrior) tells the villagers how to defeat Nian, whose weaknesses are loud noises, fire, and the color red. That stated, I took some liberties with the legend. For example, in many versions, Nian is presented as a beast, monster, or dragon. Chinese dragons, unlike Western dragons, are auspicious. In my version, Nian is an evil dragon. I chose to make Nian evil and be defeated by a clever girl protagonist, who transforms Nian into a symbol of good luck and fortune. Most significantly, I created Mei. Mei, pronounced "may," means "beauty." It is also my Chinese name. Like Mei, I was born in the Year of the Dragon. Unlike other versions, the hero in my story is female. I really wanted a female heroine because . . . well, girls rule!

— Virginia

I am full of gratitude for the women warriors in my life.
This book is dedicated to my mentors and best buds, Dr. Barbara Moss and Dr. Rafaela M. Santa Cruz.
Thank you for guiding my career in academia. You are the magical warriors who have inspired me to be a powerful dragon-slayer.
—Virginia

To Savannah, Wren & Sparrow
— Tim

Library of Congress Cataloging-in-Publication Data.
Names: Loh-Hagan, Virginia, author. | Banks, Timothy, illustrator.
Title: Nian, the Chinese New Year dragon / written by Virginia Loh-Hagan ;
illustrated by Timothy Banks.
Description: Ann Arbor, MI : Sleeping Bear Press, [2020] | Summary:
An illustrated retelling for young readers of the Chinese folktale about a
dragon that threatens a village each spring and Mei, the young girl who is
destined to defeat him.
Identifiers: LCCN 2019004063 | ISBN 9781585364138 (hardcover)
Subjects: | CYAC: Dragons--Folklore. | Chinese New Year--Folklore. | Folklore--China.
Classification: LCC PZ8.1.L936 Ni 2020 | DDC 398.2 [E] --dc23
LC record available at https://lccn.loc.gov/2019004063